Hangin' With
Hilary Duff

by jo hurley

Scholastic Inc.

New York   Toronto   London   Auckland   Sydney
Mexico City   New Delhi   Hong Kong   Buenos Aires

Photo Credits:
Cover (front): Stewart Volland/Retna Ltd.; (back) Paul Beauchemin/Retna Ltd. Page 4: Giulio Marcocchi/ABACA; Rudolphe Baras/London Features Int'l; Page 7: Jim Spellman/ WireImage.com; Page 8: Stewart Volland/Retna Ltd.; Page 9: Chris Polk/FilmMagic.com; Page 10: Everett Collection; Page 11: Everett Collection; Page 13: Tribune Media Service Int'l/ABACA; Page 14: Everett Collection; Page 15: (top) Everett Collection, (bottom) Mathew Imaging/FilmMagic.com; Page 16: Photofest; Page 17: Photofest; Page 18: Everett Collection; Page 19: Everett Collection; Page 20: (top and bottom) Everett Collection; Page 21: (left)Everett Collection, (right) Jim Spellman/WireImage.com; Page 22: Rudolphe Baras/London Features Int'l; Page 24: Everett Collection; Page 25: Evan Agostini/Image Direct/Getty Images; Page 27: Kelly A. Swift/Retna Ltd.; Page 28: ABACA; Page 29: ABACA; Page 30: (left) Paul Smith/Feature Flash/Retna Ltd., (right) Kevin Mazur/WireImage.com; Page 31: (left) Lionel Hahn/ABACA, (right) ABACA; Page 32: Chris Polk/FilmMagic.com; Page 33: Chris Polk/FilmMagic.com; Page 34: Chris Polk/ FilmMagic.com; Page 35: (left) Chris Polk/FilmMagic.com, (right) Jim Ruymen/Corbis; Page 36: Jeff Kravitz/ FilmMagic.com; Page 37: Jeff Kravitz/Corbis; Page 38: Rudolphe Baras/London Features Int'l; Page 39: (top) Paul Smith/Feature Flash/Retna Ltd., (bottom) Rufus F. Folkks; Page 40: ABACA; Page 41: (top) Bill Davila/ FilmMagic.com, (bottom) Evan Agostini/Image Direct/Getty Images; Page 43: ABACA; Page 44: ABACA; Page 45: Tammie Arroyo/Retna Ltd.; Page 46: Krista Niles/Associated Press,AP; Page 47: Rudolphe Baras/London Features Int'l.
Photo Editor: Sharon Lennon

ISBN 0-439-61732-4
Copyright ©2003 Scholastic Inc.
All rights reserved. Published by Scholastic Inc.
SCHOLASTIC and associated logos are trademarks and/or registered trademarks of Scholastic Inc.

12 11 10 9 8   4 5 6 7 8 9 /0

Design by Louise Bova
Printed in the U.S.A.
First printing, October 2003

contents

say hello to hilary duff, a real-life 'tween queen!

Ready to step into a fairy tale? Hilary Duff's life is filled with the stuff of dreams: a successful TV show, blockbuster movies, hit records, and even her own fashion line! From her humble roots in Houston, Texas, to big-screen stardom in Hollywood, one thing is certain: this Duff has *all* the right stuff.

Born to perform, Hilary (or Hil, as her friends call her) started out in showbiz dancing and acting in local commercials. When mom Susan Duff saw that her youngest daughter had stars in her eyes, she packed up and moved the family to Los Angeles to try their luck. After a few key TV and video roles, Hil hit it way big with the title role in the Disney series *Lizzie McGuire*. From there, Hil landed parts in several feature films, including *Agent Cody Banks* and the #1 big-

Hilary Duff, 'tween queen extraordinaire!

screen Lizzie movie. Now Hil's set to star in a modern update of the Cinderella story, which sounds about right! This 'tween queen has all the keys to the kingdom — and she's only just begun her rise to the top.

Inside this mega-cool scrapbook, you'll find out what Hil really thinks about the biz and learn why she switched gears from acting, to writing and recording her own CD, *Metamorphosis*. Enjoy page after page of picture-perfect, red-carpet pinups, plus sizzling details on Hil's past, present, and future. From Hila-raves to Hila-rants, this super-starlet has some secrets to share about her love of animals, her obsession with clothes, and her very own Prince Charming.

You'll find out what it takes to be a real 21st century princess when you're hangin' with Hilary Duff!

Hilary is all smiles.

little girl, big dreams

Hilary was only three years old when she begged to wear the same red shoes every day. She knew what she wanted — to dance! At the young age of six, Hil became a dancer in a Columbus Ballet Met touring company production of *The Nutcracker*.

When Hilary and her sister Haylie (two years older) were enrolled at a private performing arts school in Texas, Hil would tag along for Haylie's acting classes. Soon Hil decided she wanted to try acting, too!

THE MOMENT WHEN HILARY KNEW SHE WAS BORN TO ACT:

"My mom, Haylie, and me came out to California and Mom got all these books on show business. We were staying in this one-bedroom apartment and going on like two hundred auditions. When friends came to visit they would say, 'You have a nice house in Houston — why are you living *here*?' But I was determined. When I want something, I really want it!"

WHERE'S DUFF DADDY?

Although Bob Duff doesn't live in L.A. with his girls, he visits Hil, Haylie, and Susan every couple of weeks. He stays at the house in Houston, where he manages his own chain of convenience stores.

TOP SECRET!

At first when her mom asked Hil if she wanted to act, Hil replied, "No way, that's stupid!" But she changed her mind — fast — when she saw how much Haylie loved performing.

DID YOU KNOW?

Haylie was the first Duff to get a real Hollywood acting role. She appeared in a TV movie called *Hope* (1997). That was the event that prompted Mama Duff to take her two girls west to L.A. to try their luck at other auditions. At the time, Hil was just finishing up fourth grade.

Looking pretty in peach—Hilary Duff's got talent and style.

the 411 on the 'tween queen

name: Hilary Ann Duff

nickname: Hil

birthdate: September 28, 1987

star sign: Libra

birthplace: Houston, Texas

current residence: Los Angeles, California

parents: Mom, Susan; Dad, Bob

siblings: One sister, Haylie (she's two years older)

pets: Two dogs, L'il Dog and Remington

best friend: Taylor (from home in Texas)

height: 5'5"

hair: Brown/Blond

eyes: Brown

right or left: She's a righty

talents: Dance, singing, acting, and all kinds of sports

school: She has a tutor full time when she's working

secret ambition: To be a superstar! Hey, she's certainly on her way. . . .

act one, scene one: learning the ropes

Although the early days in L.A. were tough, Hilary kept smiling through her auditions! Soon, she landed herself a few key roles. And as time went on, the gigs got bigger . . . and bigger . . .

hilary duff's ^early hollywood résumé

1997
TV MOVIE: *True Women* with Rachael Leigh Cook

1998
DIRECT-TO-VIDEO: *Casper Meets Wendy* (Wendy)

Hil says: "There were all of these special effects and I learned how to fly!"

1999

TV MOVIE: *Soul Collector* (Ellie) — Hil won an award for this! Best Supporting Actress, Young Artist Award.

2000

TV GUEST STAR: *Chicago Hope* (Jessie Seldon in episode called "Cold Hearts")

2001

FEATURE FILM: *Human Nature* with Tim Robbins (Young Lila Jute) She played a younger version of Patricia Arquette's lead character.

Peekaboo! Hilary takes a look at stardom for the first time.

hil's big break: lizzie mcguire

Soon, Hilary landed the big gig of all time: a lead role on a new Disney television series called *Lizzie McGuire*. According to Hil, she was super-intimidated at auditions. She went back five or six times before she was cast in the role of Lizzie.

ARE LIZZIE AND HILARY ANYTHING ALIKE? SORTA!

Hil explains: "In the first episode, [Lizzie] talks about how she's not a jock, a rebel, or a diva, but she's a 'none-of-the-above' . . . . She's not really comfortable in her own skin." In real life, Hil says she's not really shy like that. She relates more to the *cartoon* Lizzie because "she's sassy . . . . [and] edgy."

A surprise hit packs a punch! "I was totally shocked at the success of the TV show. I had been auditioning for about four years to get parts here and there. Then I got Lizzie and now people see me at the mall and say, 'Hey, I like your show.' It's cool to know you are a part of something that people like."

FUN FACT

Surprising Lizzie fans include Steve Tyler from Aerosmith (he guest-starred on an episode playing Santa Claus); comedian Wayne Brady; and *Saturday Night Live*'s Jimmy Fallon.

A comedy about how to survive the crushes, cliques, and crises of middle school, Lizzie McGuire premiered in 2001 on the Disney Channel.

Hil as Lizzie with her cartoon alter ego.

friends-n-family... forever-n-ever

One of the coolest parts about playing Elizabeth Brooke McGuire — aka Lizzie — is working with the talented cast on the show, including Robert Carradine, who plays her dad, Sam; Hallie Todd, who plays her mom, Jo; and Jake Thomas, who plays her super-annoying brother, Matt.

FUNNY FACT

Adam Lamberg, who plays the role of David Zephyr "Gordo" Gordon, auditioned for Lizzie with two broken wrists — and casts on both of 'em. That's one way to be remembered!

Hil and her *Lizzie* costars Adam Lamberg (Gordo) and Jake Thomas (Matt) cheer on their winning show at the Nickelodeon Kid's Choice Awards.

lights, camera, movies!

In 2002, as *Lizzie McGuire* started growing in popularity, Hilary was handpicked to star in a made-for-cable movie called *Cadet Kelly*. In the cable flick, Hil played the role of Kelly Collins, an artistic, fashion-conscious gal whose life flips upside down! Her new, retired general stepdad uproots the family from the city and sends his step-daughter to George Washington Military Academy in upstate New York. That sounds, like . . . so un-Hilary!

Hilary shined as Kelly Collins, a reluctant cadet.

At the Academy, new Cadet Kelly butts heads with everyone, including her squad leader (played by Christy Romano, star of *Even Stevens*). She also falls for an upperclassman (played by Shawn Ashmore of *X-Men* fame). Will she desert the ranks — or stick it out?

Cadet Kelly was the #1 highest rated movie ever shown on the Disney Channel!

up on the big screen: agent cody banks

In 2003, Hilary had a supporting role in the hit movie, *Agent Cody Banks*, alongside *Malcolm in the Middle* star and Hil's off-the-set pal, Frankie Muniz.

The character of Natalie Connors is way different than *Lizzie McGuire*! In the movie, Natalie's dad is the super scientist doing research on nanotechnology that spies want to steal! But Natalie's fearless. She's the popular girl who's super-independent. Sounds a lot like the *real-life* Hilary Duff!

Hilary shares a moment with costar Frankie Muniz.

TOP SECRET!

How did Hilary snag the part of Natalie? Just say thanks, Frankie! According to Hil, Frankie Muniz told her about the role when he guest-starred on Lizzie McGuire.

ON MAKING AN ACTION-ADVENTURE FILM:

"This movie is crazy! It's action-packed! Every single day on the set there were these big explosions . . . there was this one part where one of the bad guys kidnapped me. We ran outside and he was getting ready to throw me in a car and I climbed up the side of the car so he couldn't get me. It was really fun!"

**Hilary gets smart and serious as Cody Banks'
main squeeze, Natalie Connors.**

the lizzie mcguire movie
ciao, roma! lizzie goes italian

The Lizzie McGuire Movie debuted in spring 2003 in the #1 slot to great reviews and lots of raves for Hil's acting and singing.

"GOOD-BYE LIZZIE MCGUIRE, HELLO FABULOUS!"

Hil had double the fun on this flick! She plays *two* roles: the part of Lizzie (of course) AND the part of Isabella (in a brown wig and Italian accent!)

THE PLOT:

Lizzie and her pals pack up for a class trip to Italy. While there, Lizzie gets mistaken for an Italian pop star named Isabella. While Isabella's out of town, her singing partner Paolo convinces Lizzie to help him perform at the International Video Awards. The result: a perfect princess transformation for Lizzie.

Here, Paolo's taking Lizzie for a ride on his Vespa.

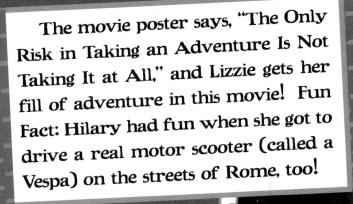

The movie poster says, "The Only Risk in Taking an Adventure Is Not Taking It at All," and Lizzie gets her fill of adventure in this movie! Fun Fact: Hilary had fun when she got to drive a real motor scooter (called a Vespa) on the streets of Rome, too!

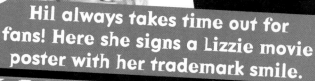

Hil always takes time out for fans! Here she signs a Lizzie movie poster with her trademark smile.

THE BEST THING ABOUT FILMING A MOVIE IN ROME:

THE PIZZA! Hilary says she ate pizza twice a day and started going through pizza withdrawal when she returned home.

cheaper by the dozen
whoa – meet hilary and her eleven brothers and sisters!

Hilary stars in this comedy remake of a 1950s classic, *Cheaper by the Dozen*.

In the movie, Hil plays Lorraine Baker, one of *twelve* kids. Whew! When her dad gets a big-city football coaching job, he packs up his wife and eleven of the kids and moves everyone in together. Now that's cramped quarters! Where will Hil hang all her outfits?

Hil's joined on the big screen by actor Tom Welling (*Smallville*) and actress Piper Perabo, who play her older siblings. Other cast members include MTV *Punk'd* star Ashton Kutcher, rapper Missy Elliot, and the actor/comedian Steve Martin.

WHAT YOU MAYBE DIDN'T KNOW:

The original *Cheaper by the Dozen* took place at the turn of the 20th century. Boy, have things changed since then!

TOP SECRET!

The part of daughter Lorraine was written especially for Hilary.

cinderella story
someday my prince will come . . .

So, will Hil's prince ever really come? THIS may be the movie. Set in Southern California's San Fernando Valley, this is the story of how one nerd turns into the total babe. As everyone knows — that isn't easy. But if anyone can tackle the task, it's Hilary Duff!

A *Cinderella Story* costars Shane West (from *A Walk to Remember*), Rupert Grint (Ron from the *Harry Potter* movies), and Carmen Rasmussen, a former contestant on 2003's *American Idol* show.

HILARY EXPLAINS WHY THIS ROLE IS DIFFERENT FROM HER OTHERS:

"It's a bit of a plain-Jane part, and no one has ever seen me like that before. The character has to deal with her dad dying and the awful family environment she is growing up in. Then she has a metamorphosis and changes. I am really looking forward to that challenge."

Move over, Kirsten Dunst — Hilary's here! The pop princess has earned a big raise in the few years as she's watched her fame skyrocket. With *A Cinderella Story*, Hil gets two million bucks — plus. Yup, that'll buy a whole LOTTA pink flip-flops.

TOP SECRET!

Hil's mom Susan is also a producer on the film.

tune up! makin' music

Not only does she act . . . but this girl can sing! How did Hilary get interested in singing and writing songs?

"My sister was in a band and I saw them rehearsing one day and it looked like so much fun. I thought, 'Hey, I wanna do that!' So I started taking classes . . . got a really great music manager . . . started taking some voice lessons . . . That's basically it."

Ho, ho, ho! Hil duets with L'il Romeo on "Tell Me a Story," a song from her holiday album.

Thanks to the fans, Hil's hottest tunes reach the top of the charts — and get regular rotation on MTV. She even got to host *TRL*!

FUN FACT

Hil not only sings on her records — but she writes some of the music, too!

Hil practices singing in front of the mirror with a hairbrush. Don't you?

Hil's superhit "I Can't Wait" went platinum and her video "Why Not?" got heavy rotation on MTV. She even got to host *TRL!*

MUSICAL NOTE

✺ Who was Hilary caught hangin' with for a special DVD release of *The Lion King?* Hil joined Raven, Orlando, Christy Romano, Anneliese, Kylah Pratt, A.J. Trauth, and Tia, Tamera, and Tahj Mowry on a Disney all-star singing version of "Circle of Life."

the times they are a-changin'
hil's new, solo album: metamorphosis

IN HER OWN WORDS . . .

"Music is something I'm just dipping my toes in. It's totally new, so that's kind of what the 'metamorphosis' is about."

"The recording studio is so much more relaxed. It's really, like . . . chill. Performing is a whole different thing. I get so nervous."

"[The album] is not really pop music and it's not really hardcore rock. It's somewhere in between. I'm not doing any collaborations . . . but my sister [Haylie] is going to be doing a little bit of singing with me."

"Acting is not me at all, I'm playing somebody else. That's what cool about singing. It's more personal — it's all about me. I think singing will be a little more complicated but I love it."

Hilary belted out "The Tiki, Tiki, Tiki Room" on a Disneymania album that also featured singing phenoms 'N Sync, Christina Aguilera, Usher, and others. Here, Hil hits a few high notes with Lance Bass from 'N Sync.

life according to hilary

ON FAMILY

My sister [Haylie] is an amazing young woman with morals and values and inner strength that I see daily. My mom and dad are, too. They have always lived what they teach."

"My mom goes along with me every time I go out of town and every time I work she is there."

"[Haylie and I] do everything together and she's my best friend. We fight and bicker, usually about 'You stole my clothes!' or 'You stole my makeup!' It makes me sad to see that some of my friends aren't so close with their siblings . . . we are both really supportive and close."

ON FRIENDS

"It's hard because I go out of town so much and I don't really have a lot of time to spend with my friends, but they understand that I'm working and I love to work. And when I'm back in Texas, I see them all the time."

Hil chats with a friend.

ON AUDITIONS

"You have to handle rejection really well, because you might go on seventy auditions before you book anything. You can't take it to heart."

ON DREAMS

"Never, ever give up on your dream. If you are a kid, have family behind you all the way. Study your craft and respect those who have gone before you."

ON BEING FAMOUS

"Being recognized makes it harder to go places. But it's so much easier to be nice to people than it is to be rude."

FUN FACT

In the new Duff digs in California, Haylie lives in the guesthouse out back — so the sisters still get to spend a lot of time together!

Hil and Haylie at home—having fun with crafts.

ON BEING A ROLE MODEL

"Mom always tells me and my sister, 'You know who you are looking up to but you never know who may be looking up to you.' I think that's important."

"I get fan mail that says, 'You're my role model' . . . and it makes me feel really good, but I'm not saving lives here. I love acting, I love what I do, but I think [kids] should be looking up to people like doctors or scientists or presidents that have changed the world in some way."

she's so stylin'

spotlight hilary: on the red carpet

She likes mixing it up — pretty or punk! Does Hil like to shop? "Of course, I love all that girl stuff!"

Hil says, "I love clothes. I can't control myself. I have a huge fetish for shoes and clothes and makeup. I'm the kind of person who doesn't like to wear things over and over again."

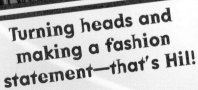

Turning heads and making a fashion statement—that's Hil!

Hil and fellow 'tween queen Amanda Bynes present a 2003 MTV Movie Award together.

Pretty in pink or funky in stripes . . .
it's all part of the Duff look!

※ Hilary is launching her very own clothing line called *Stuff by Hilary Duff*! She's moving into stores in a big way in spring 2004. Hil proudly says, "I'm actually helping design the styles, pick the fabrics and colors together with two cool fashion designers . . . they really want to capture my style and ideas."

※ Hil's line of products includes way more than just clothes! She's bringing out her own makeup, journals, picture frames, and much more . . .

※ Disney launched a major line of *Lizzie McGuire* clothes featuring Hilary's superstar image.

※ What a doll! Hilary has her very own fashion doll, too — with three outfits you can change.

AND THE AWARD GOES TO . . .

※ Nominated for Favorite TV Actress (2002 and 2003) in Nickelodeon Kids' Choice Awards. The show was voted best TV series, too!

※ Young Artist Award for Best Supporting Actress in *Soul Collector*

※ 2002 Radio Disney Music Award for "Best Style"

※ Nominated for three 2003 Teen Choice Awards: Movie Actress — Comedy; TV Actress — Comedy; and Female Hottie.

※ *The Hollywood Reporter* named Hilary as one of the top three ranked showbiz kids.

NOW APPEARING . . . EVERYWHERE!

Hil's appearing on the cover of major magazines (*Disney Adventures*, *Popstar*, *Teen*, and *Vanity Fair*, just to name a few). She guest-gigged on *Star Search* as a judge and co-hosted *Access Hollywood*.

where the boys are!

THE PERFECT GUY

"He has to be tall, pretty tall. He has to make me laugh and he has to be smart. He can't spend more time in front of the mirror than I do."

THE BOYFRIEND

On Aaron Carter, who Hilary's been dating on and off since she was thirteen: "We both had busy schedules. When I was shooting the TV show, he was constantly on tour promoting his album. It's tough to have a public relationship and there are always all these rumors."

THE TV CRUSH

What about Clayton Snyder, who plays Lizzie's space-case crush, Ethan Craft? He looks like an ideal love match for Hil — he's tall (6') with eight pets (parrots and turtles among them). He's funny, too — loves Monty Python movies. Hmmm. Who knows?

Hil and Aaron get close...

THE COSTAR

On Frankie Muniz, cutie-pie and super spy star of *Agent Cody Banks*: "We've known each other for a long time. I think I met him right when he was filming the pilot for *Malcolm in the Middle*. It's cool because we're kind of the same age, but I'm bitter that he can drive already and I can't!"

Hil and costar Frankie Muniz at the premiere of *Agent Cody Banks*.

...at the premiere of *The Lizzie McGuire Movie*.

REAL-LIFE MAJOR ATTRACTIONS

MAJOR CRUSH: Hil admits to crushing on Josh Hartnett — big time!

MAJOR HOTTIE: She thinks soccer star David Beckham is just dreamy . . .

MAJOR CONNECTION: Freddie Prinze Jr. called up Hil when he penned a script with a part he wrote specifically with her in mind.

all for a good cause

Hilary says, "Whenever we have a dinner party or birthday party, [my mom] tells people, 'Don't bring presents for us, bring diapers or something so we can give it away.' I think this influence from my parents started it for me and my sister. It's really important to give back."

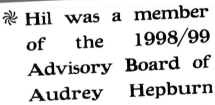

❋ Hil was a member of the 1998/99 Advisory Board of Audrey Hepburn Children's Fund and also supports the charity group Ocean of Love, dedicated to helping Ocean County, New Jersey, children with cancer and their families.

❋ Both Hilary and her sister Haylie are members of the Committee for Kids With a Cause — a non-profit kids' organization whose mission is to help kids who suffer from sickness, poverty, lack of education, abandonment, neglect and/or abuse. Other members: Hil's costars from TV's *Lizzie McGuire*, Ashlie Brillaut (Kate) and Clayton Snyder (Ethan).

DID YOU KNOW?

Hil's dogs L'il Dog and Remington were both rescued from animal shelters?

✳ Hilary met the legendary Nelson Mandela as well as Kofi Annan, Secretary-General of the United Nations. How? She participated in a United Nations conference for teen leadership programs.

✳ Hil often tries to visit hospitals when traveling for work. "We get groups together from less fortunate homes who have never been able to go to a theme park and we just hang out and act like normal kids. We also get food for them and clothes."

Hilary Duff is a HUGE animal rights advocate. Hil says, "When I was four or five, I wanted to be a veterinarian, but then as I got older I figured out they had to do sad things like put animals to sleep. I decided I didn't want to do that anymore."

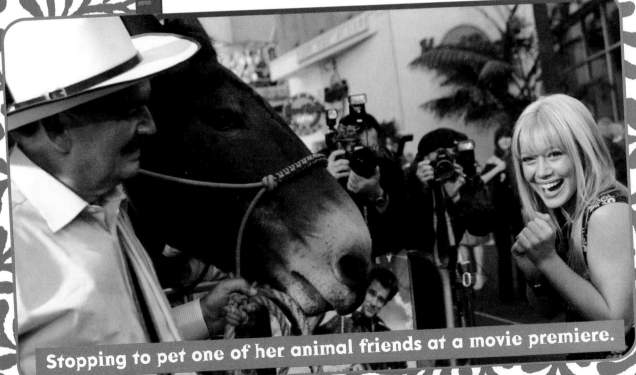

Stopping to pet one of her animal friends at a movie premiere.

faves, raves, and rants!

hil's faves

A healthy Hilary is a happy Hilary.

FOOD: This supergirl loves almost everything! "Because I am from Texas my favorite food is Mexican food! But I also love sushi, Thai, or Italian food . . . or just a regular burger . . . and pickles . . . and any kind of candy . . ."

SPORTS: swimming, tumbling, Rollerblading, jumping on her trampoline, and Tae Bo

BOOKS: The *Harry Potter* books, *Holes* by Louis Sachar, and anything by Shel Silverstein ("when I was really young I used to memorize the poems")

TUNES: All kinds of music — hip-hop, some pop, rap and rock including No Doubt, Boomkat, Good Charlotte, Eminem, Nelly, Blink 182, Vanessa Carlton and many more.

POP STARS: Britney! "I used to be obsessed and I still think she is really cool. Britney's beautiful."

TV SHOWS: *7th Heaven* and *Gilmore Girls*

VIDEO GAMES: "In my free time I play Sims on my laptop . . . I got totally hooked on it . . . now I'm getting everybody around me hooked as well."

ACTRESSES: Sandra Bullock, Cameron Diaz, and Susan Sarandon ("I think she's just a special person inside.")

DREAM GUEST STARS ON HER TV SHOW: Drew Barrymore, Britney Spears, or Julia Roberts

FASHION FIX: Really high heels

FASHION COLLECTION: Louis Vuitton hand-bags (she also collects picture frames, shoes, and hats)

HAIR STYLIN': Sebastian products like Potion 9 and Power Glam hairspray; and Dumb Blond by Tigi shampoo and conditioner

MAKEUP: MAC eyeliner, blush, and Studio Fix powder

LIP GLOSSIN': Nars, Lancome, and Juicy Tubes

WHERE SHE SHOPS: On Melrose Avenue in L.A. and the Beverly Center ("because they have tons of cool stores like Jami Lynn, Wet Seal, and Rampage")

JUST FOR FUN: yo-yo tricks, walking on her hands

IN HER FREE TIME: Likes hangin' with friends best of all

Hil shows off her patriotic side.

hila-raves . . .

HOLIDAYS AT HOME IN TEXAS: "I get to go see my family, eat a lot of food, and enjoy my Uncle Mike's homemade ice cream — yum!"

HER POSSE: "The people I am working with are my mom Susan, my theatrical manager Susan, and my music manager Andre, who are all very protective of me — and make sure I get my rest and get time to see my friends."

HER WILD AND WONDERFUL FANS: "Some fans told me they were dressing up like me for Halloween. I was like, whoa. That's pretty crazy."

THE ULTIMATE ROLE MODEL: "I wish I could have met Princess Diana."

Hilary is flying high!

hila-rants . . .

SHE LOVES HER PET PUPS, BUT WHAT ARE HER PET PEEVES? "Chipped nail polish and wastefulness."

WHY CAN'T TABLOIDS AND GOSSIP JUST GO AWAY? According to Hil, "When you say things to magazines . . . it comes out two months later and everyone thinks that when they read it, they're reading it as if it happened that day."

DUMB LUCK! While filming in Rome, Hil's tutor Marsha broke her ankle . . . and then when she went to film in Vancouver, Hil's new tutor broke her toes! Talk about a bad break for Hil's study habits!

NOT THE FLU! When Hil's feeling under the weather, she stays in bed and drinks a lot of tea and water.

CALLING ALL KLUTZES! "The other day I hurt myself falling down the steps. And I do stuff like that all the time!"

HOW EMBARRASSING! When working on her first movie, the director asked her to "hug the couch" as she walked by. But Hil didn't know that was director-speak for "stay close to the couch." So she leaned over and hugged it!

WHAT'S *REALLY* TUFF FOR DUFF? Being spotted in public. "I can go to malls but it's hard. If I'm in a rush and I want to go to certain stores, I can't. And it makes it worse if you wear a hat or scarf because then people really say, 'Oh, that's HER.'"

Hil with her fans on *TRL*.

a day in the life of duff

What would it be like to have a camera crew follow you around all day? If you spent a day with Hilary Duff, you'd discover an ordinary girl doing extraordinary things!

Hil says, "People think [my life] is so different from regular life and I don't think it is at all. I just go to do my job. After work is done, I go home and do my chores and make my bed and do my homework. So acting is kind of like a sport to me. Like, all my friends play sports and I work on a TV show."

TAKE NOTE:

Just last year, Hil's October schedule included traveling to Paris, then to London to accept an award at the Disney Channel Kids Awards (a UK special event), and THEN to Rome to film *The Lizzie McGuire Movie*.

how does this 'tween queen stay soooo normal?

SCHOOL: Hilary has a tutor every day from 9 am to 2 pm (reduced to 3 hours — instead of 5 — when she's making movie). "I get a good education because it's just me and my teacher, one-on-one."

Hilary in her room at home: She's a girl like any other . . . except that she's also a superstar!

HER CHORES: Making the bed, taking the trash out, feeding the dog. Just like YOU.

AW, PHOTO SHOOT! Sometimes Hil has back-to-back sessions in front of the camera for magazines and other promotions like Got Milk?; *Popstar* magazine; *Disney Adventures* magazine — and many more. Whew! How does she find the time?

HER WORK SCHEDULES: "When you are working on a TV show, everything goes really fast. You might do four scenes a day and then you do hair and makeup and then you have wardrobe fittings and then you go to school. Then when you do a movie it's slower, you might only do one or two scenes a day and there's a lot of sitting around and waiting."

Homework time!

CATCHING SOME Z'S: Depending on work schedule, Hil's bedtime is usually about 10:30 — but later if she can stay up with friends, especially on weekends.

ON BURNOUT: "Sometimes I won't even know what I'm doing the next day and I'll just have to go do it and be told right before I run on. But I tell my mom when I'm tired and burned out. I'm like, 'Mom, I need a break,' and she's like, 'Okay, cool."

THE FAN FACTOR: "I get around two thousand questions a day (on my website) and since I'm working nine hours a day I only have time to answer a few."

Hilary actually filmed a real twenty-five minute "Day in the Life" profile with moments from her home life, personal style tips, and behind-the-scenes look at the video for her hit song, "Why Not." "A Day in the Life of Hilary Duff" can be seen on VideoNow personal video players from Hasbro.

P.S.

Her website actually reports more than 375,000 e-mails weekly . . . AND Hilary has also received more than seven million fan notes on the Disney site . . . AND she gets more than 300,000 fan letters per month! But she still wants to take part of every day and give back to everyone who writes and e-mails. No wonder she has so many fans!

into the future

what's next?

Hil says she may star in a cool girl action movie ("like a teenage *Charlie's Angels*") . . . she's reportedly filming *Confessions of a Teenage Drama Queen*, another major flick . . . and oh yeah, she is also going to her friend Tori's spring formal, of course! Hil always tries to put family and friends first!

In 2003, she appeared as herself on *The George Lopez Show* and *Good Day L.A.*

in five years?

"I want to be in college, keep working at movies, singing, my clothing line . . . Hopefully it all works out."

in ten years?

"I hope to still be pursuing what makes me happy . . . whatever that is."

hil's ultimate goals

"To do my best, to be a good friend, to leave the world a better place, and to enjoy every second."

get in touch!

For the latest on Hil's life and all that . . . check out her website regularly at www.hilaryduff.com. She keeps an ongoing journal for fans — with news from all her trips around the country — and the world. Plus, on her site you can send questions for her to answer. Of course, she can't get to all of them — but give her a shout-out anyhow!

You can also send fan mail to Hilary at her official fan club:

HILARY DUFF FAN CLUB
3702 S. Virginia St. G12 #487
Reno, NV 89502